R0201459120

09/2020

PALM BEACH COUNTY
LIBRARY SYSTEM
3650 Summit Boulevard
West Palm Beach, FL 33406-4198

Welcome to The GROW & READ Early Reader Program!

The GROW & READ book program was developed under the supervision of reading specialists to develop kids' reading skills while emphasizing the delight of storytelling. The series was created to help children enjoy learning to read and is perfect for shared reading and reading aloud.

These GROW & READ levels will help you choose the best book for every reader.

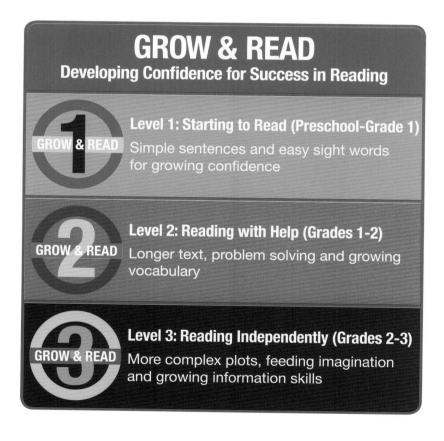

GROW & READ
Developing Confidence for Success in Reading

GROW & READ 1

Level 1: Starting to Read (Preschool-Grade 1)
Simple sentences and easy sight words for growing confidence

GROW & READ 2

Level 2: Reading with Help (Grades 1-2)
Longer text, problem solving and growing vocabulary

GROW & READ 3

Level 3: Reading Independently (Grades 2-3)
More complex plots, feeding imagination and growing information skills

For more information visit growandread.com.

Copyright © 2020 by Fabled Films LLC

All rights reserved. No part of this book may be used or reproduced in any manner whatsoever without written permission from the publisher except in the case of brief quotations embodied in critical articles or reviews. For information address Fabled Films LLC, 200 Park Avenue South, New York, NY 10003. info@fabledfilms.com

Published by Fabled Films LLC, New York

ISBN: 978-1-944020-34-7

Library of Congress Control Number: 2019955049

First Edition: May 2020

1 3 5 7 9 10 8 6 4 2

Cover Designed by Jaime Mendola-Hobbie
Jacket & Interior Art by Josie Yee
Interior Book Design by Aleks Gulan
Typeset in Stemple Garamond, Mrs. Ant and Pacific Northwest
Printed by Everbest in China

FABLED FILMS PRESS
NEW YORK CITY
fabledfilms.com

For information on bulk purchases for promotional use please contact Consortium Book Sales & Distribution Sales department at ingrampublishersvcs@ingramcontent.com or 1-866-400-5351.

The
Weeping Wombat

by

Tracey Hecht

Illustrations by
Josie Yee

Fabled Films Press
New York

Chapter 1

The moon was bright.

The stars were sparkling.

It was a beautiful night.

But Walter the wombat did not care.

Walter was sad.

"I feel terrible!"

Walter said to himself.

Walter's head hung low.

Walter's shoulders sagged.

"I feel like this weeping willow tree,"

Walter said.

Walter whimpered and Walter sniffled.

Whimper.

Sniffle.

Whimper.

Sniffle.

"I wish the other wombats
wouldn't make fun of me."

"So what if I cried when I lost my whistle . . .

And when I was feeling lonely . . .

And when I got that splinter.

So I'm a little bit weepy!

What's the big deal about that?"

Walter whimpered and
sniffled some more!

Along came Dawn, Bismark, and Tobin.

"I hear a whimper,"
Tobin said.

"And I hear a sniffle!"
Bismark said.

"I think it is coming from over there,"
Dawn said.

Dawn pointed across the meadow
at the weeping willow tree.

Chapter 2

Dawn wiggled her head

through the willow branches . . .

And saw one very weary wombat.

"Walter," Dawn said.

"What are you doing under here?"

Tobin and Bismark wiggled their heads through the willow branches, too.

"Why, Walter!" Bismark declared. "You look positively woebegone!"

"Tell us what's wrong," Tobin said.

Walter lifted his head.

Walter wiped his eyes.

But when Walter opened his mouth to speak,

all that came out . . .

was one . . .

LOUD . . .

"Walter, why don't you come out

from under this willow,"

Dawn said.

"We can all go sit by the

woolly violets."

Dawn pulled the branches wide

so that Walter could waddle out

from under the willow tree.

Walter felt wary.

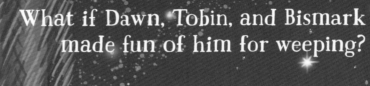

What if Dawn, Tobin, and Bismark
made fun of him for weeping?

Worse, what if Dawn, Tobin, and
Bismark called him wimpy, too?

Walter wavered.

"Come on, Walter!" Tobin said.

"We can walk over there together!"

Tobin took Walter by the paw.

"Well, okay," Walter agreed.

Walter was starting to feel

a little bit better already.

Chapter 3

Walter sat down beside the woolly violets

and looked up at Dawn, Tobin, and Bismark.

They were waiting for him to speak.

Walter's eyes welled up with tears.

 "The other wombats tease me for weeping,"

Walter whimpered.

"They say I am **weak**.

They say I am a **wimp**.

They call me Walter the Weak and
Wimpy Wombat Who Weeps!"

"Say what?"
Bismark declared.

"The other wombats
tease you for weeping?

Why that's just wackadoodle!"
Bismark exclaimed.

"Weeping is not wimpy," Tobin agreed.

"Walter," Dawn said.

"Do I look **weak?**"

Walter looked at Dawn and **wrung** his paws.

"And does Tobin look **wimpy?**"

Walter looked at Tobin and

wrinkled his brow.

"And what about Bismark?" Dawn asked.
"Does Bismark look like he **weeps?**"

Bismark **winked,** and gave
Walter his most **winning** smile!

Walter laughed. "No," Walter said.

"Bismark does not look like he weeps.

And Tobin does not look like a wimp."

Walter's head hung low again.

"And you do not look weak," he added.

"Well, guess what, Walter?" Tobin said.

"We're all weak and wimpy and
weepy sometimes!"

"It's true, Walter," Dawn said.

"Sometimes we all cry."

"I never cry," Bismark said.

"Except when I'm missing my

old grandpa Guffy . . ."

Bismark
sniffled.

"Or when the thunder is extremely loud . . ."

Bismark
whimpered.

"Or when I have

very . . .

sad . . .

feelings trapped inside me!"

Bismark started to **wail!**

Chapter 4

"You see, Walter," Dawn said.

"Weeping is just another way

to show how we feel."

"Like laughing,"
Dawn said.

"Or clapping!"
Tobin said.

"Or sniffling!"
Bismark said.

Dawn smiled at Walter.

"Weeping is nothing to worry about.

In fact, sometimes weeping

can make you feel better."

Bismark stopped weeping.

Bismark thought about this.

"Why, Dawn," Bismark said.

"I think you are right!

I do feel better!

In fact, now I feel **wonderful**."

"So I'm not a wimp?" Walter said.

"And I'm not a weakling?

And weeping is just another

way to show how I feel?"

"Yes!" Bismark cried out.

"And will you look at what I found here!"
Bismark exclaimed.

Bismark reached down into the

woolly violets and picked up a whistle.

"A whistle to celebrate your

wonderful wombat self!"

"My whistle!" Walter said.
"You found it."

Walter took the whistle, but then . . .

Walter started to weep some more!

"What's wrong now?" Tobin said.

"Not a thing," Walter exclaimed.

"Now I am weeping because I am happy!"

"And it does feel **wonderful!**"

And with that,

Walter wrapped his arms around

Dawn,

Tobin, and

Bismark.

And gave them all a big,

walloping, wombat hug!

Grow & Read Storytime Activities
For The Nocturnals Early Reader Books!

Download Free Printables:

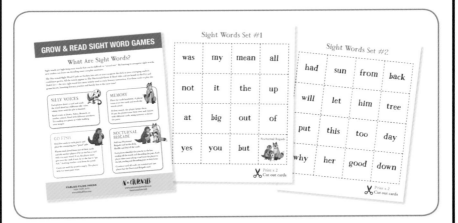

Sight Word Games

Brigade Mask Craft and Coloring Pages!

The NoCTURNALS

FUN FACTS!

What are The Nocturnal Animals?

Pangolin: The pangolin is covered with keratin scales on most of its body except its belly and face. A pangolin sprays a stinky odor, much like a skunk, to ward off danger. It then curls into a ball to protect against attack. Pangolins have long, sticky tongues to eat ants and termites. Pangolins do not have teeth.

Red Fox: The red fox has reddish fur with a big, bushy tail and a white tip. Red foxes are clever creatures with keen eyesight. They have large, upright ears to hear sounds far away.

Sugar Glider: The sugar glider is a small marsupial. It looks like a flying squirrel. It has short gray fur, black rings around its big eyes, and a black stripe that runs from its nose to the end of its tail. Sugar gliders have special skin that stretches from the ankle to the wrist. This special skin allows sugar gliders to glide from tree to tree to find food and escape danger.

Wombat: Wombats have poor eyesight but make up for it with great hearing and a keen sense of smell. The wombat is a marsupial. Like many marsupial animals, female wombats have a pouch that holds their young. But a wombat's pouch, unlike that of most marsupials, opens to the rear, which protects their young since wombats enjoy digging and being underground. They are also known for constructing elaborate tunnel systems in deep sand.

Nighttime Fun Facts!

Nocturnal animals are animals that are awake and active at night. They sleep during the day.

About the Author

Tracey Hecht is a writer and entrepreneur who has written, directed and produced for film. She created a Nocturnals Read Aloud Writing Program in partnership with the New York Public Library that has expanded nationwide. Tracey splits her time between Oquossoc, Maine and New York City.

About the Illustrator

Josie Yee is an award-winning illustrator and graphic artist specializing in children's publishing. She received her BFA from Arizona State University and studied Illustration at the Academy of Art University in San Francisco. She lives in New York City with her daughter, Ana, and their cat, Dude.

About Fabled Films & Fabled Films Press

Fabled Films is a publishing and entertainment company creating original content for young readers and middle grade audiences. Fabled Films Press combines strong literary properties with high quality production values to connect books with generations of parents and their children. Each property is supported by websites, educator guides and activities for bookstores, educators and librarians, as well as videos, social media content and supplemental entertainment for additional platforms.

fabledfilms.com

FABLED FILMS PRESS
New York City

Read All of The Grow & Read Nocturnal Brigade Adventures!

This series can help children enjoy learning to read and is perfect for shared reading and reading aloud.

Great For Kids Ages 5-7

Level 1

Level 2

Level 3

Visit nocturnalsworld.com to download fun nighttime activities
#NocturnalsWorld